AF291391

I'm
(aLMosT)
ALWAYS KIND

Designed by Nicola Butler
Cover design by Lucy Wain

Usborne Publishing, Usborne House, 83-85 Saffron Hill, London EC1N 8RT, England
Usborne Verlag / Usborne Publishing Ltd. Prüfeninger Str. 20, 93049 Regensburg, Deutschland, VK Nr. 17560

My mummy told me that being KIND is the most important thing in all the world.

"More important than being the fastest runner?" I asked. "Or than knowing all the answers?"

"Even more important than those," she said.

"Then it is very lucky," I said quickly, "that I am ALWAYS kind."

Being KIND means...

...helping my little sister
reach things from
a high shelf...

...tidying away
the breakfast
things...

...trying to cheer
people up when
they feel sad.

But sometimes when I am kind,
it doesn't work out the way I want it to...

Why did she look so sad when I gave her a nice compliment?

Why was Mr. Williams so cross about me being kind to snails?

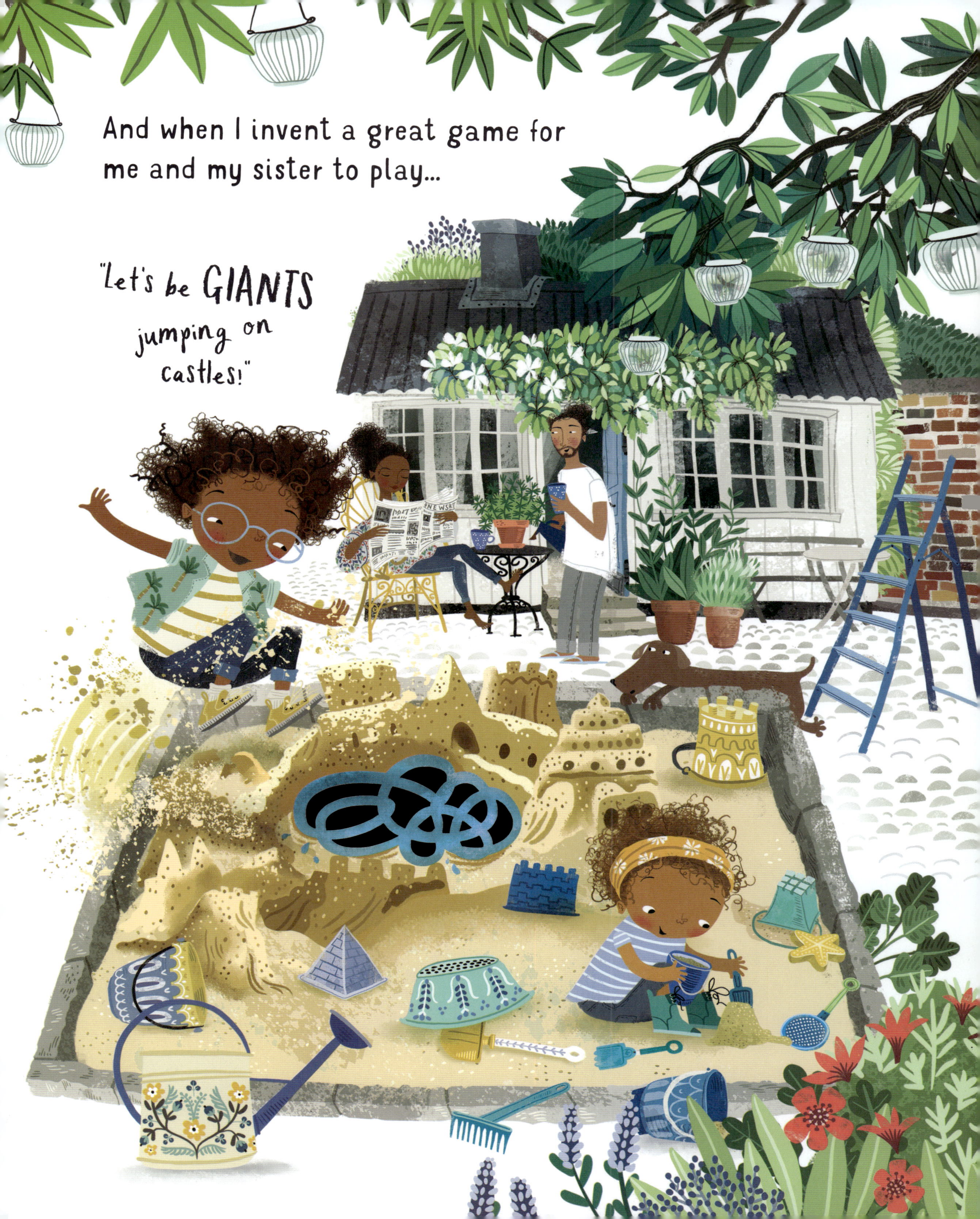

And when I invent a great game for me and my sister to play...

"Let's be GIANTS jumping on castles!"

...she screams,
"WAAAAAAAH!
YOU'RE SO MEAN!!!"

And I feel mad
and bad and sad.

I ONLY
meant to
be KIND.

I helped fix my sister's sandcastles. And afterwards,
I told Mummy that I hadn't meant to be mean.

Mummy understood. "But what YOU think is nice isn't
always the same as what someone else thinks is nice.
Sometimes, to be kind to someone, you have
to walk around in their shoes first."

So I tried it...

It didn't work.
Now I didn't feel like being
kind to ANYONE.

Mummy wasn't cross. She smiled instead. "I didn't mean REAL shoes," she said. "I meant trying to put yourself in someone else's place. If you imagine how they might feel, you might see what could make them happy."
"I'm sorry about your shoes," I told her.

She gave me a hug, and it unscrumpled my feelings and made ME feel happy...

Mummy is KIND.

"This is what it feels like when someone is kind to you," I thought. So I decided to try again.

Before I put snails on Mr. Williams' garden the next day,
I tried to imagine how he feels about his garden.

He LOVES those flowers.

So I thought it might be kinder to look after them.

When I thought of a fun game to
play with my sister, I tried imagining
how she might see it first.

What would she think of a great,
big water fight...?

If I was in her place, I guess I wouldn't want all my paintings to get soaking wet...

sploosh!

So instead I said,
"Shall I play too?" (Even though
I could think of games
I'd rather play.)

But after I painted pictures with my sister,
she played lots of my favourite games with me.

"Being kind is GREAT," I thought.

But some people are hard to be kind to...
At school, I found the new kid sitting on her own. She looked
really grumpy. Everyone else was playing and having fun,
so I sat down by her and asked, "Do you want to play tag?"
"No," she said.
"Skipping?" I asked.
"NO," she said.

In the end I said, "I want to be kind to you,
but I don't know how... What will make you happy?"
She looked at me. "I like football?" she said.

So we played football.
And she started to smile.

So did I.

Then I realised something.
Being kind doesn't just make OTHER people happy...

It makes
YOU happy too!

Kindness makes you feel warm and sunshiney.
And when you feel that way, you feel like
being kind to someone else.

So the kindness
gets
passed
on...

And it makes THEM feel warm and sunshiney,
and they feel like being kind to MORE people!

"Happy Birthday!"
"I'll give you a hand."
...sunshine-kindness spreads...
EVERYWHERE.
THANKS!
"Are you lost?"
"Here you go."
ET WELL SOON

"This will help you feel better."
WELCOME!
"Thanks!"
"Can I help carry your parcels?"
GO!

Being kind is sometimes easy and sometimes hard. But it's really important to try.

And because it's the imPORTant-est thing in the world,

I am (almost) always KIND.